Shadow

Jill Newsome

Illustrated by Claudio Muñoz

A DK INK BOOK
DK PUBLISHING, INC.

To Isabel

DK Publishing, Inc.
95 Madison Avenue
New York, New York 10016

Visit us on the World Wide Web at http://www.dk.com

Library of Congress Cataloging-in-Publication Data

Newsome, Jill.
    Shadow / Jill Newsome : illustrated by Claudio Muñoz. — 1st ed.
        p.   cm.
    "A DK Ink book."
    Summary: After moving to a new home, a little girl is unhappy until her pet rabbit
Shadow helps her to make a new friend.
    ISBN 0-7894-2631-5
    [1. Moving, Household—Fiction. 2. Rabbits—Fiction.
3. Friendship—Fiction.] · I. Muñoz, Claudio, ill. II. Title.
PZ7.N48664Sh   1999   99-13450
[E]—dc21   CIP

The illustrations for this book were created with watercolor and India ink.
The text in this book is set in 26 point Bell MT.

Color reproduction by Dot Gradations, U.K.
Printed and bound in China by L. Rex Ltd.

First American Edition, 1999

2 4 6 8 10 9 7 5 3 1

Published simultaneously in the United Kingdom by Dorling Kindersley Limited.

My name is Rosy.
Everything was fine—
my home, my school, my friends.
Until the day we moved.

That day,
my whole
world turned
upside down.

Nothing I did seemed
right anymore. People
started to say how rude
and bad-tempered I was.

Every day Dad walked me to my new
school through the woods behind our
new house. It was dark and spooky,
and I didn't like it one bit.

Everyone at my new school looked so strange, I wished I was really tiny so I could hide in my dad's arms.

There were nights when I just couldn't go to sleep. My dreams were scary. How I missed all my friends and my old home!

One day snow was falling
so school closed early.

We walked home slowly,
watching the silent woods
in the swirling snow.

All of a sudden, I saw a
little face – a rabbit lying
quite still, looking at me.

I saw that it was hurt, so very carefully
I picked it up and carried it home.

Everyone agreed the rabbit could stay.

Mom helped me take care of
the rabbit's hurt leg.

Dad helped me make a cozy hutch for its new home.

Before long, the rabbit was feeling well
enough to hop around the house. It followed
me everywhere, so I called it Shadow.

Shadow was
very brave.
He ran after the cat
and even after the dog.

We played
hide-and-seek
together. We
had lots of fun.

But one day Shadow disappeared.
I looked in every room in our house
and all over the neighborhood.

At suppertime, I wasn't hungry.
All I could think about was how
much I missed Shadow.

What would I do without my new friend?

Suddenly, I had an idea.

I got some paper
and began
to write:

lost
white rabbit
called Sl

Just then, the doorbell rang.
It was Nancy, a girl from my
class, holding a huge box.

Inside, there was Shadow!

Now Nancy and I walk to school together.
We play at each other's houses and in the
woods, which are not spooky anymore.

And sometimes
Shadow comes, too.